# Busting the
# BIG APPLE
# BANDIT

## The ADVENTURES of AMOS and KAREENA LEENA FOGLEY

### by DAVID M. LONG

*To A4, Mr. No No, and Cute Face:*

*"Courage, Not Cowardice"*

CHAPTER 1

# Climbing Coffin

"Why did I agree to this?" Murphy Maxwell moaned as he nervously paced back and forth waiting for the elevator in the lobby of New York City's Empire State Building. "What if the elevator cable snaps? What if we get stuck and I start making panic noises that sound like a wounded water buffalo?" **Curse you, Amos!!"**

Clearly, Murphy had a bad case of sky-scraper-itis. Every fifteen minutes, he dashed from the elevator line straight to the little boys' room just seconds before his overactive sprinkler system let loose. I swear that knucklehead has the world's smallest bladder.

Rising 102 floors straight up the spine of this steel skyscraper sounded awesome. I'd never been in a building this tall. Back home, I'd climbed to the 12th floor of the Valley Springs Bank. As part of a summer science experiment, I wondered how far a paper airplane would travel from that height. I launched that bird straight out over the hustle and bustle of Main Street.

**Altitude** (noun): *springing high off a diving board increases your altitude so you can drop like a cannonball and splash the flirty lifeguards playing kissy face.*

On the sidewalk below, Ol' Mrs. Shindledecker shuffled toward the post office to buy the new Elvis stamp. For 40 years, Mrs. Shindledecker ran the Valley Springs Sewage Plant which explained why she was always in a stinky mood. And as luck would have it, my paper airplane started running low on fuel, dropping in altitude, and racing like a missile straight at Mrs. Shindledecker's forehead.

She never saw the paper airplane coming. Pow! I heard the thud from above. Poor Mrs. Shindledecker screamed, "Aliens attacking! Call the President! Call the Army and Navy and every mall cop in the city!" I laughed until my sides hurt.

Anyhow, back to the Empire State Building lobby. I love adventure, but stuffing Murphy into that elevator, or "climbing coffin" as he called it, would be a real

**Covert** (Adjective): *anything done in secret like sneaking up on a friend with your paint ball gun, shooting him in the rear end, and making him howl like a coyote*

challenge. Thankfully, my sister Kareena Leena thought up a <u>covert</u> plan.

Recently, Kareena Leena took up jump roping as a hobby. She earned enough money working at Mr. Bolinbaugh's bowling alley to buy her own jump rope. Mr. Bolinbaugh paid her a nickel for every pair of bowling shoes she squirted with foot fungus spray. It was a rotten job, but Kareena Leena made the most of it. To pass time, she wrote a rap called "Yo, No Cooties on the Footies."

Jumping rope didn't come easy for Kareena Leena. On her first attempt, she tripped on a sidewalk crack and plunged face first into the trash cans at the end of the driveway. When

> **Wreckage** (Noun): *whatever is left (i.e. scratched seat, crooked handlebars, etc.) after your little brother accidentally plows his bike headfirst into the dumpster behind the grocery store.*

she rose from the <u>wreckage</u>, Tuesday's egg salad oozed down her face and a moldy peanut butter and jelly sandwich stuck to the side of her leg. **YUCK!**

But over the last few weeks, Kareena Leena's jumping really took off. She taught herself to Double Dutch using two jump ropes. Murphy and I twirled what looked like whirling spaghetti noodles while Kareena

Leena repeatedly bounced without tripping. Watching her sometimes made me dizzy, but it mostly made me hungry watching those noodles twirl all over.

**Instincts** (noun): *whenever you get the heebie jeebies or creepy crawlies down your spine because you know something funky is about to happen*

As part of our covert plan to trap Murphy in the elevator, we transformed her jump rope into a lasso. My secret agent <u>instincts</u> told me that Murphy might bolt for the nearest street exit when the elevator finally opened on the first floor. Kareena Leena stalked Murphy while I rigged up a lasso knot I learned at last summer's Grundy County Fair. There, I met a cowboy named Freddy, but all the locals called him Fast Fingers. He could lasso a calf in less than four seconds, draw his pistol with lightning speed, and he never got caught in elementary school for picking his nose.

And just as I finished the sliding knot, the elevator dinged. It was go time! Murphy's ears perked up just like my dog Doodle's do when my mom starts her blow dryer. And sure enough, Murphy's next move was a sprint for the street door exit. With the speed of a Pronghorn Antelope, Murphy zigged and zagged through the lobby as if running through the grasslands of East Africa.

I hoisted the lasso above my head and twirled it in a way that would make Freddy Fast Fingers proud. I slung the rope straight at Murphy's size four sneakers and ....missed. Uh, I not only missed, but I missed really badly. **Uh-oh!**

Instead of heading toward Murphy, the jump rope sailed straight at the lobby's security officer who I later learned was New York City's Muscle Man of the Month for March. He didn't carry a gun. He didn't need to with the guns he packed inside both of his bulging sleeves.

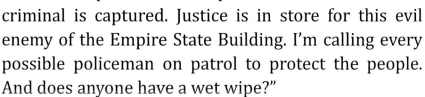

While Officer Muscles McGuire slurped on a very, very, very hot cup of coffee, I yelled, "Duck!" But it was too late. A coffee bomb exploded in his face and he screamed, "I will not sleep until this crazy criminal is captured. Justice is in store for this evil enemy of the Empire State Building. I'm calling every possible policeman on patrol to protect the people. And does anyone have a wet wipe?"

Thankfully, Kareena Leena stayed calm. She wouldn't let Murph escape. And after watching a recent episode of Global Gallopers, she knew exactly what to do. The only way to catch the world's second fastest animal was to become the world's first fastest animal...a cheetah. And I don't mean a cheetah like someone who doesn't play by the rules. I'm talking about a cat cheetah. **Prrrrr!**

"So you wanna race do you, Mr. Murphy the Pronghorn Antelope? Well, meow, meow," Kareena Leena whispered while taking cover behind an Empire State Building welcome sign. She crouched like a cat, sniffed the air, and even purred a little. As Murph sprinted for the lobby's exit, Kareena Leena sprung from her hiding spot and pounced on him from the rear.

While riding on his back and clawing her recently manicured fingernails into his neck, Kareena Leena threatened, "Get in the elevator or this cheetah has Murphy burgers for dinner!"

Surrendering was Murphy's only option, and he willingly entered the elevator. I dove between the closing doors and off we went to the top of the Empire State Building. We were safe, but not for long.

CHAPTER 2

# Dude on the Roof

The elevator exploded upward, racing to the top of the Empire State Building. And, like always, whenever Murph's nerves act up, he rattles off random facts. "Did you know that the Empire State building was completed in 1931 and was the first building ever to have over 100 stories? It sits smack dab in the middle of New York City at the intersection of West 34th Street and 5th Avenue." Thankfully, the elevator traveled so fast that Murph ran out of time before completely annoying us. **Phew!**

The elevator slowed and the doors opened gently. We made it to the top! Kareena Leena skipped out and greeted New York City's never-ending <u>skyline</u> with a big ol' smile. "Hello, Big Apple," Kareena Leena shouted as she cartwheeled around the observation deck. The view

**Skyline** (noun):
*Even if you spread your eyeballs in opposite directions, you won't be able to see all the buildings that line the New York City sky.*

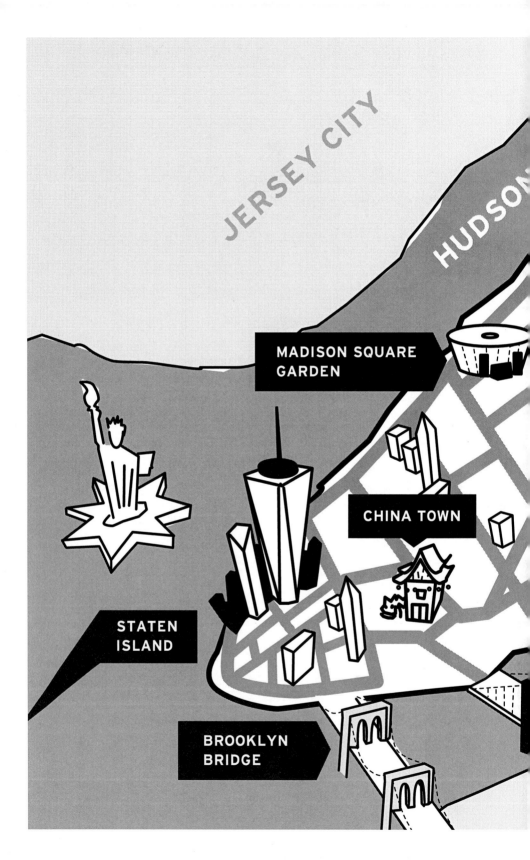

was amazing. We could see all the different sections, or boroughs, of the city: Brooklyn, Queens, The Bronx, Staten Island, and, of course, the most famous, Manhattan.

**LaGuardia Airport** (proper noun, pronounced la-gward-i-a): *airport named after Fiorello La Guardia, the mayor of New York City in 1953*

To the east, hundreds of airplanes played Follow the Leader on the runway of LaGuardia Airport. To the north, itty bitty people rollerbladed, jogged and enjoyed horse drawn carriage rides through the quiet of Central Park. And to the west, the end of the Hudson River rushed straight into the New York Harbor.

As we looked to the south, Kareena Leena let out a shriek similar to that of a South American Howler Monkey. I thought someone stepped on her pig tails in the middle of a cartwheel. "Guys, guys, I see her, I see her!" Kareena Leena squealed. "I see the Statue of

Liberty. She's waving at me. What's up, girl!? Friends, Romans, countrymen, lend me your tired, your poor, your huddled messes who can't breathe." Kareena Leena was a little off on the words to the Statue of Liberty Song, but I always appreciated my little sister's enthusiasm.

Murph remained in the elevator as long as possible and finally worked up the courage to test out his wobbly legs. He packed his new *Zoom Zoom 4.1 Night Vision Binoculars* hoping to record various <u>urban</u> observations. Murph wondered if urban areas still contained wetland groups such as a marsh or swamp. He also hypothesized that city noises such as car horns, busses, trains and construction could impact the nesting habits of the city's pigeons.

Kareena Leena wasn't the least bit interested in pigeons, but Murph's *Zoom Zoom 4.1 Night Vision Binoculars* might be fun to play with. Murph kindly loaned Kareena Leena the Zoom Zooms and she quickly zoomed in on Lady Liberty's armpit. "Hey, guys, does anyone know if Lady Liberty wears deodorant? With her arm waving high in the air, I don't want her having stinky pits." **P.U!**

> **Urban** (adjective): *anything inside a city like skyscrapers, shoppers and traffic jams that cause your dad's face to turn red and yell at you*

Next, Kareena Leena gazed below at Times Square. Times Square is an area of Manhattan where millions of people cram into every New Year's Eve. They gather to watch the New Year's Eve ball drop down a pole high atop a Times Square building.

As the ball drops, people count down the final seconds. When the countdown ends, everyone yells, "Happy New Year!" Confetti drops from the sky, horns blow, and some people actually smooch which is super gross. I have no idea why adults enjoy smearing their germs on each other. **Icky!**

Kareena Leena kept scanning Times Square below and let out yet another yelp. "Kareena Leena, are you looking for more stinky armpits?" I questioned. "No, no, Amos. There's a dude climbing up the Times Square building!"

I ripped the Zoom Zooms from her hands for a closer peek and sure enough, I could see a figure gracefully climbing the side of the building. Using supersonic suction pads that stuck to the windows, he slowly inched his way to the top. He dressed in all black, wore a mask, and packed a bunch of gadgets hanging from his backpack. What was he doing? **Hmmmm?**

We tried telling some adults but they were too busy posing for pictures.

And, none of them spoke English. New York City hosts thousands of conventions every year and this group just arrived from Sweden for the 79th Annual Meatball <u>Convention</u>.

**Convention** (noun):
*A large meeting of people who enjoy the same stuff like meatballs, cars, or science fiction people who believe there's life on planet Nit Wit*

Using the Zoom Zooms, I took another look. The figure on the building removed tools from his backpack. Using a wrench and a screwdriver, he loosened some bolts that fastened the New Year's Eve ball to the pole. Quickly, he threw sections of the ball into his backpack and that's when I knew he wasn't a repair man doing annual maintenance. He intended to steal the most famous ball in the world!

I yelled out to the gang, "Circle the wagons, cowboys, we have a Big Apple Bandit on our hands!" Kareena Leena was the first to join my huddle. "Amos, this is terribly exciting. Count me in. Let's do this. Nothing can stop us. Uh, but wait a minute. What are we doing and what's a bandit?"

"Oh brother, Kareena Leena," I scolded as Murphy soon joined the group. "A bandit is a thief, a criminal, an enemy of good who we must bring to justice. That dude on the roof is a Big Apple Bandit. If we don't stop him, New Year's Eve will be ruined for millions of people!"

"Roger that, Amos," Kareena Leena confirmed. "I'll call the police and tell them a Band-Aid™ is on the loose."

"Kareena, it's a bandit, not a Band-Aid™, you ding-a-ling, and we don't have enough time for the police. Head for the elevator now!" I commanded.

We sprinted to the first available elevator heading down, and when the doors opened, terror gripped us. There stood Muscles McGuire. He lunged from the elevator, grabbed me around the neck, and said, "Stop, you sneaky drink spiller. I'm sending you straight to the New York City slammer."

I couldn't breathe. My entire body went limp, and my life flashed before my eyes. **flash!**

CHAPTER 3

# Courage, Not Cowardice

Thankfully it wasn't my life flashing before my eyes, but rather the cameras flashing from the Swedish Meatball Gang. Apparently, Swedish people all get along really well and the country has a very low crime rate. Maybe since they're so nice, they should be called "Sweet-ish." So, when they saw me in a headlock and gasping for air, they snapped pictures of a rare crime scene.

Well, I owe the Swedish Meatball Gang a big favor because their camera flashes completely blinded Muscles McGuire. Instinctively, he shielded his eyes, and without realizing it, he released me from his death grip. This saved me from having to go Kung Fu crazy and use my spinning tornado kick on his private parts. **Hee Yah!**

As Muscles McGuire rubbed the stars in his eyes, Murphy, Kareena Leena, and I jumped into an opening elevator and dropped 102 floors to first floor. As we started leaving the Empire State Building lobby, Kareena Leena drifted off toward some lady pushing around a drink cart selling tea and coffee.

"Kareena Leena, what are you doing?" I screamed. "Muscles McGuire is going to throw us all in the slammer and you're ordering a drink?"

In a thick British accent Kareena Leena calmly replied, "Fiddle sticks. My britches are in <u>shambles</u> from this afternoon's <u>shenanigans</u>, and I need some hot tea to make me feel all luvvly-jubbly again."

> **Shambles** (noun): *dropping a glass will leave it in shambles. Slacking off in school will leave your report card in shambles.*

> **Shenanigans** (noun): *crazy and often naughty action like when a kid at school puts a dead frog in some girl's lunchbox*

My jaw hit the floor. The police are chasing us. The Big Apple Bandit is on the loose, and my sister is off in La-La Land talking like the Queen of England and drinking tea like an old granny.

"Listen, Kareena Leena," I uttered with great maturity. "Acting like royalty isn't exactly my cup of tea so get your legs moving."

"Oh, Amos, relax. I met a sweet girl named Matilda on the elevator. She's from London and is visiting New

York City. Her accent is totally cool, and we decided to be pen pals. Don't worry, I'm ready to go catch the Big Apple Bandit now." **Carry On, Chap!**

Only five city blocks separated us from Times Square, but the sidewalks on Broadway Avenue were jam packed. We cut over on West 34th Street knowing it would take a miracle to reach the Big Apple Bandit before he finished stealing the ball. We needed help.

"Amos, let's hail a taxi," Murphy suggested. "New York taxi drivers are the best." And before I even moved, Kareena Leena sprinted to the curb with her arm held high. In her best New Yorker accent, Kareena hollered, "Yo, taxi! My fellas here need a ride. Get us to Times Square and don't give me any lip!"

We piled into the backseat. The driver's name was Mr. Mushtaq. He didn't speak English very well, but man could he drive. He rocketed straight north on 7th Avenue shouting,

"Rapido, rapido!" Mr. Mushtaq's instincts must have told him we were on a covert mission to save the city. Kareena Leena let out a squeal similar to the taxi's tires as we zipped around busses, delivery trucks, and a guy crossing the street dressed up as Elvis. He must have been out celebrating the new stamp Mrs. Shindledecker liked.

"Yes, yes, rapido" I agreed. Mr. Mushtaq made up for lost time and restored our hope in catching the Big Apple Bandit. At the intersection of 7th Avenue and West 42nd Street, Mr. Mushtaq slammed on his breaks, crashed into the curb, gave us a thumbs up and said, "Okey, dokey?"

"Rock on, Mr. Mushtaq," Kareena Leena declared giving him a five dollar bill, two breath mints, a keychain, and everything else in her pocket.

Standing on the sidewalk, we peered upward to the top of the Times Square Building. We could still see the Big Apple Bandit stuffing the last few pieces of the New Year's Eve ball into his backpack. His getaway was near, but not if we could stop him.

The bandit scooted to the edge of the Times Square building and blew a big bubble. He must like bubble gum. And then to our surprise, he jumped right off the side. I expected him to be the Big Apple Pancake three seconds later, but a parachute blasted out of his

backpack and off he floated down 42nd Street directly to the Hudson River. He must have a getaway boat stationed on the water. I felt helpless. Our chance to catch him was literally drifting away. **Noooo!**

Just then, we heard a friendly voice say, "Whatcha doing me brother and sista? Don't look so sad." Standing next to us was this cool-looking Jamaican guy with long braided hair. He wore a bright green and yellow shirt with baggy shorts and sandals. His name was Samuel and he offered us a ride in his <u>rickshaw</u>. Samuel's easy going personality calmed us down. We knew he could help, so we hopped in.

**Rickshaw** (noun):
*a light two-wheeled cart that holds sightseers while a super duper strong guy pedals them around*

"Follow that parachute!" I yelled with new hope. Samuel replied with a cool, "Okay, mon," and off we went like a lightning bolt. Samuel told us he participated in the Olympics as part of the Jamaican bobsled team so speed was the name of his game. And he was right. We gained on the parachute and spotted the Big Apple Bandit landing near the water.

> **Accomplice** (noun):
> *If you distract your mom while your brother steals a cookie, you are the accomplice, or person helping with the crime.*

And sure enough, the Big Apple Bandit had an <u>accomplice</u>. He landed right on top of a submarine anchored along the river. His friend opened the hatch, pulled in the bandit, and slammed the door shut.

Samuel peddled his rickshaw until the front tire touched the Hudson River. We could almost grab the submarine but it sank beneath the water too quickly. The Big Apple Bandit was gone.

> **Cowardice** (noun):
> *when your bravery tank is running on empty and you feel like a big wimp*

Samuel looked at me and with a tender face and whispered, "Courage, not <u>cowardice</u>, young mon."

Samuel was right. New Yorkers are tough. When buildings fall over, they rebuild them. When hurricanes hit, they clean up the mess.

It was time for me to tap into this New York spirit. **Man up, Amos!**

CHAPTER 4

# City of Heroes

At this point in the story, you may be wondering how we ended up in New York City. A few months ago we watched an episode of my favorite television show called *Global Gallopers*. In the episode, Dr. Giggles travelled to New York City hoping to learn more about the Rock Pigeon's habitat. Turns out, <u>immigrants</u> brought pigeons to America in the 1600's as a food source. And since most people don't study pigeon history, they aren't aware of the heroic acts of America's first pigeons.

> **Immigrant** (noun): *a person who permanently moves to a new country. Some consider the English arriving on the Mayflower to be America's first immigrants.*

On the morning of December 13, 1711, on a farm in a city called New Amsterdam (which later became New York City), a group of pigeons gathered together.

They griped and groaned about their rusty cages and longed for fancy meals such as sunflower and bacon-flavored thistle seed. One of the young pigeons decided it was time to take matters into his own claws. His name was Peter.

When Peter was a young squeaker, many of his fellow pigeons picked on him for being small and nicknamed him <u>Smidgeon</u> the Pigeon. But as the years passed, Smidgeon's courage grew. And on December 15, Smidgeon led The Great Pigeon Rebellion of 1711.

> **Smidgeon** (noun):
> *mixing a smidgeon, or small amount, of baking soda with vinegar produces a volcanic chemical explosion. Try it, but ask your mom first.*

Early that wintry morning, eleven year old Hans Van Franz walked to his barn to feed Smidgeon and the rest of the pigeons. Halfway to the barn, Hans stepped in a steaming pile of horse manure putting him in a rather foul mood. He finally reached the barn only to notice that every pigeon was lying face down in their cage. ***Shhhh!***

Thinking they were dead, he opened the cage's door. As

it swung open, Smidgeon the Pigeon gave the command, "3-2-1 liftoff!" In bird language it sounded more like, "Coo, coo, coo, coo-coo!" And in an instant, twenty-five pigeons fluttered out the barn door and into the free skies above. Hans van Franz tried catching them, but gave up after Smidgeon shot him in the eyes with one last squirt of bird doo doo. And that's how pigeons arrived in New York City.

And now that Murphy knew all this pigeon history, he just had to visit New York City. We thought that convincing my dad to take us might be a challenge, but to our surprise, he jumped at the chance. My dad is one-sixteenth Swedish so once he heard about the 79th Annual Swedish Meatball Convention, he was more than willing to tag along.

**Appliance** (noun): *any contraption, device or gadget that has buttons and lives in your kitchen*

Plus, my cousin lives just outside New York City in a town called White Plains and we could sleep in his attic apartment for free since my dad is a tightwad. My cousin's name is Tyler Fancy, but we call him Bud. Bud Fancy is an <u>appliance</u> salesman who only works five hours per week, but still makes gobs of money. Bud is super fun because he makes animal noises with his armpit and rides to work on a 30-year-old moped.

With our lodging all set, we headed straight to the

**Perturbed** (adjective): *being upset, like when the pitcher on the other team plunks you in the back with a baseball*

Valley Springs depot and caught the first train to New York City. Murphy counted all the stops through Ohio, Pennsylvania, and New York. All in all, we stopped 65 times. I'll be honest, I was getting a little <u>perturbed</u> with all the stops and of course Murphy brought an encyclopedia and sprayed facts the entire time. "Did you know people refer to New York City as the Big Apple, but no one really knows why? Did you know the Brooklyn Bridge was the first bridge to use electricity? Did you know the borough of Brooklyn on its own could be one of the largest cities in the United States?"

On and on Murphy blabbered, until one fact grabbed my attention. He mentioned that New York City is home to many of the world's greatest people. Since 1886, New York City has thrown over 200 parades for heroes. On

June 13, 1927 New York celebrated Charles Lindbergh's first solo airplane flight across the Atlantic Ocean. After the 1936 Olympics, there was a parade for Jesse Owens who won four gold medals in track and field even though many people wished failure upon him due to the color of his skin. **Way to Go, Jesse O!**

Then he told me about the 1929 New York City Stock Market Crash. Most Americans lost all the money they kept in banks in one single day. And there was the World Trade Center collapse on September 11, 2001. Thousands of people died. And finally on October 29, 2012, Hurricane Sandy flooded streets, tunnels, subway lines and cut power around the city costing billions of dollars in damage.

And like Peter the Pigeon, New Yorkers didn't give up. They rallied. They worked hard to earn their money back. They re-built collapsed buildings. They cleaned up the mess from the flood. They showed **courage, not cowardice!**

After learning that New York City is the most courageous city in the world, my attitude changed. This was no longer a visit to New York City; it was a mission. It became my patriotic duty.

Our train finally arrived underground in Manhattan's Grand Central Station. We stepped off the train and into a sea of activity. Men and women in professional clothes hurried to work. Trains on other lines zipped past us. We hopped on an escalator, and up we rose to the city's surface. As I stepped into the light of day, my eyeballs almost popped out of my head. New York City was massive!

Bud Fancy was right there to greet us, and thankfully not on his moped. He drove a minivan and we piled in. "Welcome to The Big Apple, my family," Bud loudly greeted. And off we went weaving our way through all the craziness of downtown New York City.

As I sat in the backseat, I couldn't help but again think about all the courageous heroes who walked these sidewalks. I now travelled the streets of legends. With various monuments whizzing by, I had no idea I'd be called upon to be New York's next hero.

CHAPTER 5

# Follow That Submarine

Beneath the fast-flowing Hudson River surface, the submerged submarine plowed forward on its way to the freedom offered by the Atlantic Ocean. At that point, we could have given up, but New York City is filled with courageous heroes and now was my time to be added to the list of greatness.

Lucky for me, a ferry docked nearby. Another load of people crossing the Hudson River from New Jersey slowly made

> **Starboard** (noun):
> *a boat has four sides. The front is the bow. The right side is starboard. The left side is port and the rear is the stern.*

their way down a ramp and exited on the <u>starboard</u> side of the boat. "C'mon, guys, we have to catch that ferry!" **All Aboard!**

"Oh, Amos, that's nearly impossible," Kareena Leena doubted. "Catching fairies is like catching a hummingbird with a pair of tweezers. And we would need a flower garden filled with honeysuckle and poppies to attract a fairy."

"Kareena Leena," I yelled. "I'm talking about ferries that haul people and cars across rivers, not fairies who fly around spraying pixie dust."

"Oh, well excuse me, Mr. Twinkle Toes," Kareena Leena giggled. "I'm terribly disappointed. I had visions of my dear brother in pink tights waving a wand around in hopes of making a cute little fairy friend."

I wasn't in the mood for Kareena Leena's comedy act and sprinted to the ferry. When the last passenger stepped off, my crew boarded and scurried straight to the bridge of

the ship. The bridge is the cabin area where the captain steers the boat.

I think our frantic arrival startled the captain. "Well hold on there, my little water bugs! My name is Captain Perry P. Pottsniggle, and I run the show here on the S.S. Poop Deck. Now what's got your undies all in bunch?"

"Captain Pottsniggle," I pleaded. "Please help us. We just witnessed a bandit stealing the New Year's Eve ball in Times Square. Now he's racing out to sea in a submarine and we need a ride so we can catch him!"

## Set Sail!

"Now wait just a New York minute," Captain Pottsniggle laughed. "I've been ferrying people across the Hudson for 37 years. I've seen planes emergency land on the water. I've seen tugboats, canoes, power boats, sailboats, and even a floating school bus drift down the river. But I've never seen a submarine in these currents."

**Nautical** (adjective): *anything to do with sailing a boat, not sailing a tater tot across the school lunch room*

Murphy didn't offer much help. He was mesmerized by all the ferry's knobs, dials and buttons, all within arm's reach of the captain's chair. At Murph's fingertips were the various <u>nautical</u> instruments such as an echo sounder, global positioning system, and various electronic charts. It was all Murph could do to not touch them.

"You say there's a bandit in these waters, do you?" Captain Pottsniggle wondered. "That's hard to believe, but there's something about you young man. You have the same courage that Henry Hudson possessed when he discovered this river back in 1609."

With one last breath I pleaded, "Please, Captain Pottsniggle. I promise. We saw the bandit with our own eyes and if we wait any longer... "

"Enough said," Captain Pottsniggle interrupted. "I aim to protect the city, so let's set sail and see what we can find." He blew the horn and off we went. **Anchors Away!**

As a young man, Captain Pottsniggle served in the Navy. He told us that spotting submarines was easy if you kept a sharp lookout for big bubbles blasting to the surface.

Kareena Leena quickly interjected, "I sure hope they don't smell like the bubbles that rise to the surface when Amos is in the bathtub. Amos's famous floating bubbles smell like rotten eggs."

"Very funny, Kareena Leena," I admitted slightly embarrassed. "Keep your eyes peeled for submarine bubbles, not my bathtub bubbles."

We patrolled the New York Harbor for almost an hour with little success. In spite

> **Inquisitive (adjective):** *someone who asks lots of questions like Murphy Maxwell*

of our bad luck, I couldn't help but notice the harbor's beauty. Ellis Island popped with <u>inquisitive</u> tourists learning more about America's first immigrants who came to America for a better life. The Statue of Liberty waved to them from the south. And the New York City skyline proudly stood at attention as the world's most famous city.

Kareena Leena interrupted my patriotic moment with yet another shriek of excitement. "I see bubbles under the Brooklyn Bridge!" And sure enough, a whole gob of bubbles popped to the surface directly below the bridge.

"Full steam ahead," Captain Pottsniggle shouted. "Nobody messes with my harbor and gets away with it." Captain Pottsniggle ordered Murphy to push down the throttle and he gladly accepted his orders. The ferry's engines roared in excitement and off we went at 25 <u>knots</u> straight toward the Brooklyn Bridge bubbles.

> **Knots** (noun):
> *not a rope, but a unit of nautical measurement indicating speed, similar to miles per hour*

As we raced forward, it became clear that the submarine was in trouble. The submarine's periscope popped up and scanned the harbor for a safe spot to surface. And only moments later, the giant nose of the sub blasted to the surface as if gasping for air while submarine warning sirens drowned out the usual New York City noise.

Immediately, the escape hatch opened and two of the scariest dudes I've ever seen popped out. The first had a scar on his right cheek and a long nose like a rat. The other had an anchor tattoo on his left arm and a scraggly beard probably filled with insects or various sea critters. He didn't seem to be skipping many meals either by the looks of his roly-poly belly.

Next to pop out of the hatch was the Big Apple Bandit as if looking for a fight. Were torpedoes set to launch? Would they ram us in hopes of sinking the ferry? Fear gripped me, and I prepared for their attack!

CHAPTER 6

# Brooklyn Bridge Breakaway

Thankfully, the crew didn't attack. They were too busy gagging. It didn't take long to learn why as a wave of <u>putridness</u> floated our way. It smelled exactly like the bottom of our garbage can during a hot day in August. Wheeling that bin to the curb makes me gag every time. **Naſty!**

> **Putridness** (noun):
> *something that smells so bad you think you might lose your lunch.*

When the air cleared, we heard them arguing. "You meathead, how could you leave that sandwich sit in the engine room for a week? Letting a beautiful and delicious double-decker pastrami and corned beef sandwich go to waste should be a crime. I ought to make you walk the plank for that," scolded Commander Shaggy Beard.

For seven days, one of New York's favored sandwiches cooked in the 120-degree temperatures of a submarine engine room. Green furry mold attacked the bread. The cheese threw a stinking fit. Onion juice leaked from the wrapper. And somehow maggots found that sandwich clear in the belly of a sub. The combination of smells was like a punch to our nostrils.

"Well, gee, Commander Shaggy Beard," Petty Officer Rat Nose stated with a whimper. "I got to eatin' that sandwich and pretty soon my belly was full, and I got real sleepy. I figured I'd take a quick nap. I got all snuggly in the engine room, and when I woke up, I plumb forgot about cleaning up my leftovers."

At that point, Commander Shaggy Beard lost his last bit of patience. He reared back and punched Petty Officer Rat Nose right in the stomach launching him off the

submarine bow and into the freezing New York Harbor waters. In the process, Commander Shaggy Beard lost his balance and cannonballed right on top of his partner's head, giving him a goose egg on his pointy skull.

Thankfully, Kareena Leena knew all about nautical rescues since she took swim lessons last summer at the community pool. "Hold on, barf boys," she confidently proclaimed. "Kareena Leena is coming to the rescue before **hypothermia** kicks in!" She snatched a rope and cast it out to the two crew members.

> **Hypothermia** (noun): *when you're so cold that your blood freezes, your lips turn blue, and you start turning into an ice cube*

"Hold on and I'll pull you in!" Pulling in Petty Officer Rat Nose was a piece of cake, but hauling in Commander Shaggy Beard took all three of us. It felt like pulling in a wounded, but hairier manatee.

Once they were safely on board, Kareena Leena reached into her purse and blasted both of them with a healthy dose of perfume. "I know you fellas don't want to smell like a girl, but right now anything is better than the pail of puke you smell like." **Yucky!**

At this point, the sub floated directly under the Brooklyn Bridge. Murphy reminded us that the Brooklyn Bridge was completed May 24, 1883. "Upon completion, this suspension bridge that connects

Manhattan to Brooklyn was the largest of its kind in the world," Murph instructed us. "And a rumor that the bridge would collapse scared so many citizens that P.T. Barnum led a parade of 21 circus elephants across the bridge to prove its strength."

Little did I know that amidst the chaos, The Big Apple Bandit was preparing his Brooklyn Bridge getaway. He slipped down the side of the submarine and inflated a small rubber <u>dingy</u>. As he rowed his way to the base of the bridge, Captain Pittsnoggle shouted, "Not so fast there Mr. Big Apple Bandit! By the authority granted to me by the New York Port Authority, I order you to freeze and come aboard."

**Dingy** (noun): a small floating rescue raft that can hold 1 person, or two dogs, or five cats, or 1,563 night crawlers

The Big Apple Bandit paid little attention to the captain's orders. Instead he reached into his backpack and pulled out what looked like a rocket launcher. The Captain ordered us all to the deck floor and shouted, "Take cover. The Big Apple Bandit's packing heat!"

Taking aim at the Brooklyn Bridge, he fired the launcher sending a hook straight at the bridge's underbelly. The hook fixed itself to the steel frame and the Big Apple Bandit promptly scurried up the cable.

Midway up, the Big Apple Bandit stopped ascending for moment. Looking down at us, he shouted in a slightly

feminine voice. "You can't stop me. I'm going to steal the New Year's Eve ball. If it fails to drop, the New Year will never arrive. Time will stand still and everything will stay the same!" **Say What?!?**

So that was the bandit's motive! He was attempting to make time stand still. The world's calendars would be stuck on December 31st forever and tomorrow would never come. And off the bandit went the rest of the way, zipping to the top in only a few blinks.

There we floated in the New York Harbor. With waves splashing against our boat, it seemed our dreams of saving the city just washed out to sea.

It was in this moment of discouragement that Kareena Leena shouted, "I've got an idea!" And sure enough, my ding-a-ling sister came through in the clutch.

CHAPTER 7

# Kung Fu For You

"Circle up, goobers," Kareena Leena announced. "Ok, so last night we chowed at The Chinese Dragon Wagon in Chinatown. When I finished my yummy egg drop soup and fried squid tentacles, I cracked open my fortune cookie and the paper inside was blank. **Total bummer!** I wanted some lucky numbers or a New Year's blessing, but got nothin', nada, zilch. And that made me cry, so I headed to the ladies' room to blow my nose."

On her way to the restroom, Kareena Leena heard a growing commotion outside on East Broadway. Chinatown was alive with activity as hundreds of musicians, marchers, flag wavers, acrobats and people in dragon costumes prowled the streets in preparation for the Annual Chinatown New Year Parade and Festival.

Dagus, or large Chinese drums, pounded out a rhythm that drew Kareena Leena right out of the restaurant and onto the sidewalk.

**Nǐ hǎo** (exclamation): *a greeting that means hello in a language called Chinese Mandarin. Rather than shake hands, many Asians bow and politely say "nǐ hǎo."*

A mysterious man dressed as a South China Tiger approached her. "Well, <u>nǐ hǎo</u>, ya cute little kitty cat," Kareena Leena whispered as she reached out to pet the tiger's whiskers. **Prrrrrr!**

The man tiger didn't speak but rather forcefully reached into Kareena Leena's purse and pulled out the crumpled up paper from the fortune cookie. "Now where are your manners, Mr. Kitty Cat? You put that back or Momma's gonna call Muscles McGuire and send you to a kitty kennel."

Her words didn't faze the man tiger. Next, he pulled a purple bottle from a pouch that hung from his waist. He carefully poured some blue steamy potion over the fortune cookie paper until gradually a few letters magically appeared. He placed the paper into Kareena

Leena's open palm, smiled, and returned to the flow of the parade.

The words, "Courage, not Cowardice" appeared on the paper in big letters. And beneath the phrase appeared an address for a place called Kung Fu For You, Inc.

"That's when I knew it was a sign," Kareena exclaimed. "A New Yorker is trying to help us catch the Big Apple Bandit. If we head to Kung Fu For You, Inc., someone will be there to help. I just know it!" **Atta Girl!**

"Great work, Kareena Leena," I applauded. "You're on to something for sure. Let's head there right now."

And it just so happened that Mr. Mushtaq was in the area. We waved at his car and two seconds later he barreled around the corner. "Mr. Mushtaq at your service...again!"

"Punch it, Mr. Mushtaq, straight for Kung Fu for You, Inc. on 316 Mulberry Street!"

Like a professional stunt driver, Mr. Mushtaq raced through lanes of traffic as Murphy engaged us in what proved to be another interesting lesson on Chinatown.

"Did you guys know that there are actually six different Chinatowns within New York City?" Murph taught. "Asians from all over the world gather here speaking languages such as Chinese, Cantonese, and Mandarin adding to New York City's already diverse culture."

In no time, Mr. Mushtaq locked up the taxi's brakes in front of Kung Fu For You, Inc. "This is your exit. Okey dokey?"

"Thanks, Mr. Mushtaq. You're awesome, and we hope to see you again," I replied.

**Rigmarole** (noun): *going to a lot of fuss and effort like trying to remember everything to pack before spending the night at a friend's house. Don't forget your toothbrush!*

We stepped into the building and as soon as the door closed, all the rigmarole from the city evaporated. The peacefulness from the studio melted away all the stress from bandit hunting.

On the floor in front of us was a man in deep meditation. Sitting on a brown mat with his eyes closed, I observed his chest inhale a deep breath of air. Gently, he exhaled the same breath as if emptying not only his lungs but also any gunk clogging his soul. **Ah, Calmness!**

Murphy whispered to me, "That must be the Kung Fu Master. The Kung Fu Master has superior wisdom. Some say he can peek into your mind and read your thoughts."

**Gumption** (noun): *it's that feeling in your gut (not a trouser burp) that pushes you to take a risk.*

The calmness gave me the heebie jeebies, but I finally worked up the gumption to approach him. In my best Chinese accent, I uttered, "You speak English, Mr. Kung Fu Master? We seek help. We need lesson in bandit catching. You help us, O' Wise one?"

"Hey, weirdo," the man replied in a thick New Jersey accent. "My name's Steve, and I'm from New Jersey (he pronounced it "New Joy-zee"). I'm not the Kung Fu Master. I'm trying to take a nap after a long night loading ships down on the harbor. You must be looking for Kung Fu Master Shing. He's down in the basement. Help ya self."

We all felt a little silly mistaking New Jersey Steve for Kung Fu Master Shing, so we embarrassingly headed to the downstairs staircase. Before we took our first step, we heard a harp-like plucking noise. Of course Murphy recognized this stringed instrument. "Amos, that's a Konghou. It's a Chinese instrument played during important ceremonies."

After a couple more steps, a sweet aroma filled our nostrils. Like a <u>bloodhound</u>, Murphy snorted and sniffed, concluding the soothing scent was ginger. This fragrance has relaxed hard working Chinese people for thousands of years.

> **Bloodhound** (noun): a dog with such good smell that police and detectives will use them to solve crimes. Odor in the court!!

The staircase walls were lined with bamboo and an assortment of Chinese warrior weapons. Knives, daggers, axes, and swords the size of hockey sticks spooked us a little. With his voice trembling, Murph told us these weapons were used to chop criminals to smithereens during the Ming Dynasty back in 1368.

My palms started sweating and my throat dried up like

a desert. I could barely push out the words, "I see him. He's sitting in the middle of the room."

Just then a violent gonging noise erupted from the room, the door at the top of the staircase slammed shut, and all the lights went out. **Help!**

CHAPTER 8

# Dragon In The Dungeon?

There we stood in the pitch black staircase. No one moved a muscle. Murphy was <u>petrified.</u> "A-m-m-m-os. I c-c-c-an't hold it m-m-m-uch longer," he stuttered.

**Petrified** (adjective): *so scared your muscles lock and trap you in your own body*

Kareena Leena broke the silence first. Resembling a flamingo, she raised one leg, flapped her arms like wings and warned, "You want some of 'dis, Jersey Steve?" Kicking the air she warned, "I got some Kung Fu for you too!" **Hee Yah!**

"Pipe down my little pink ninja. You're going to hurt yourself," I scolded. I grabbed a samurai sword from the wall and instructed Murphy and Kareena Leena to follow. Our eyes adjusted to the darkness and we spotted a flickering light at what seemed to now look more like a tunnel rather than a basement hallway.

"Oh, Amos, are you sure about this?" Murphy questioned. "I think I just dribbled a little in my undies and Niagara Falls isn't too far behind!"

"Squeeze it, Murph. There's no turning back," I firmly voiced.

In a single file line, we tiptoed down the dark tunnel with my sword ready to whack any potential threat. Running our hands along the damp rocky walls provided balance and direction. Drops of water dripped from above and the damp smell reminded me of my laundry basket after my sweaty basketball clothes rotted for a week.

**Penetrating** (adjective): *finding a way inside something, like a mosquito stinger poking through your skin and injecting itchy poison*

As we moved closer, the flickering light became brighter and we felt the heat <u>penetrating</u> into the damp tunnel. "It's a fire breathing dragon!" Kareena Leena whimpered. "That scaly monster wants to roast us and serve us on top of a bed of brown rice. And brown rice doesn't match my pink sneakers."

"Would you two stop being so dramatic? Remember the fortune cookie that said Courage, not Cowardice?"

**Destiny** (noun):
*The ability to see future events before they actually happen. This ability is quite freaky.*

It's <u>destiny</u> for us to be here," I reminded them.

The tunnel narrowed, and we crawled the last ten feet. I poked my head into a dimly lit room. There wasn't a dragon in sight, but I could see a short chubby Chinese man calmly sitting with his back to us next to a fireplace.

"Amos, hurry and chop his head off, and let's get out of here," Murphy whispered.

Kareena Leena chimed in next. "That's gross, Murphy, and the sight of blood will make you faint. I say we

sneak up and give him a wedgie, smear lipstick on him, and get out of here in time to hit the shopping sales on Fifth Avenue."

Just as we prepared to attack from behind, the Kung Fu Master spoke. "My name is Shanghai Shing. I bring victory. Welcome, young apprentices. I sense in your spirit that you thirst for righteousness. How may I help?"

"Holy bamboo!" I blurted out. How did he see us? Did Shanghai Shing have eyes in the back of his head?

"Uh, thank you, Mr. Shing, here's the situation. We, we, come in peace," I mumbled.

"I know what brings you young warriors. You seek to capture Big Apple Bandit."

"Well, heavens to Betsy, Shanghai Shing. Are you able to read minds? And if you can, would you tell me if my dad is planning to buy me a cute little fuzzy hamster for my birthday?" Kareena Leena excitedly asked.

"Kung Fu Master Shing knows all. I know when you sleep. I know when you eat. I know when you pass gas in class and blame it on your classmate."

"Oh fart nugget!" Kareena Leena cried. "Shanghai Shing, I've been gassy my whole life. I try the Squeeze Your Cheeks and Release Slowly Technique in class, but sometimes the pressure is too strong, and I accidentally launch a trouser burp. And in my embarrassment, I blame Tommy Tootsalot."

"Do not worry, young warrior princess. Broccoli egg rolls do same to me so I blame Jersey Steve," Shanghai

Shing comforted. "Now let us talk busting bandit, and not busting wind. Follow me."

Shanghai Shing put all our nerves at ease. He was here to help. We followed him into another room. But before he unveiled the secret to catching Big Apple Bandits, he tested us.

Standing next to a picture of his great-great-great-great-great grandpa, Shanghai Shing stated, "My family descends from the ancient Chinese Ming Dynasty. We proud people. In 14th century, my family help make bricks to build Great Wall of China. My family stands for hard work, dedication, and an iron will."

**Mongols** (noun): *Mongolia is a neighboring country to China. They, like the Swedish, make great meatballs.*

Learning about the Great Wall perked up Murphy's ears. "That's awesome, Shanghai Shing. I have a poster of The Great Wall in my bedroom. The wall stretches over 5,000 miles, snaking its way through China. The wall is so big that it prevented the <u>Mongols</u> from invading."

"You seem very wise, Mr. Murphy. Perhaps you can help find solution to my challenge."

Shanghai Shing proceeded and pulled out a piece of wood from a cupboard. "This is bamboo wood. Bamboo leaves and shoots make yummy snack for panda bear. But bamboo wood is harder than steel. If you can break this board in half, I help you find Big Apple Bandit. If you no break bamboo board, I no help you find Big Apple Bandit."

The three of us huddled together. Using notes from his summer geometry course, Murphy suggested karate chopping the board at a 37-degree angle. Based on our hand strength, and gravitational influence, this should snap the board.

I wasn't so sure. I thought kicking it was a better option. I knew my legs were stronger than my arms and plus, my mom says I have "hammer toes" so surely one of those would shatter the board.

Little did we know that while we huddled, Kareena Leena slipped to the side. As Murph and I planned, she sprinted straight at Shanghai Shing with her

purse in hand. With the speed of a gazelle, Kareena Leena sprung into the air, whirled her purse over her head, and rammed it through the bamboo board. The wood splintered into a million pieces creating enough toothpicks for every breakfast restaurant in China. "Never underestimate a girl with a purse!"

Shanghai Shing bowed to Kareena Leena with great admiration. "Good work young warrior princess. I will now tell you the secret of bandit catching."

# CHAPTER 9

# Big Apple Bubble Gum

Mr. Shing told us this wasn't the first time a Big Apple Bandit visited New York City. Other bandits made unsuccessful attempts to cause <u>havoc</u> throughout New York's history. In

> **Havoc** (noun): *complete destruction, like Kareena Leena shattering the bamboo board into a million toothpicks*

1968, a bandit planned on kidnapping an anteater from the Bronx Zoo. The bandit's mother accused him of having too many ants in his pants, so he thought keeping an anteater in his bedroom would solve the problem.

> **Heist** (noun): *a robbery, often in a jewelry store or fancy museum with rich people paintings inside*

But the <u>heist</u> never went down. The night before the kidnapping, the bandit's mom gave him some medicine for a condition called A.D.D (or Always Day Dreaming). He took the pill, went to bed, and woke up without a single ant in his britches.

Like a true New Yorker, Shanghai Shing would never let such a villain succeed in the city he loved. He told us to follow him to another room. Stepping over all the toothpicks Kareena Leena chopped, we followed Shanghai Shing to yet another room in this never-ending basement.

We entered the dimly lit room where a spotlight illuminated a box. Carefully, Shanghai Shing lifted a black sheet covering a glass box. Inside was a pink rectangular piece of whatchamajigger. Proudly, Shanghai Shing stated, "This is secret for catching bandit you look for." **Ta Da!**

"Bubble gum?" Murphy questioned. That's right. Inside the glass box was what looked like an ordinary piece of bubble gum.

"Not just ordinary bubble gum, young boy with a bladder about to splatter!" This is Big Apple Bubble Gum containing my family's ancient Chinese secret ingredient. You see, when I was boy growing up in China, my father was scientist. He made

**Edible** (adjective): *anything you can eat like oranges and apples, not motor oil or tree bark*

ooey gooey potion using coconut milk, ginger, sugar, more sugar, even more sugar and finally <u>edible</u> rubber bands."

We further learned that when mixed with a special sap from a tree in the Shing's backyard, a wonderful <u>concoction</u> of bubble gum was created that never loses flavor, stretches like rubber bands, and doesn't stick when a bubble explodes on your face.

**Concocted** (verb): *using pieces of junk like leftover wood, nails, and glue to build your own backyard fort*

"Jackpot!" Kareena Leena celebrated. "Every time I try to break the world record for largest bubble gum bubble, Amos pops it. The splattered gum sticks to my lips, nose, and hair which is no fun for a girl growing out her bangs."

**Foreigner** (noun): *a stranger to an area like a human in a jungle or a camel in your living room*

And that's why Shanghai Shing moved to New York City. Like many <u>foreigners</u>, Shanghai Shing and his brother moved to America for a better life. With a couple of bucks in his wallet and a dream the size of Manhattan, he immigrated to New York City hoping to produce the world's best bubble gum.

"With gum that I make, no need to chase bandit. My gum so good, bandit will come to you!" Shanghai Shing stated with a smile. He removed the glass cover and quickly carved off a bubble gum sample for each of us.

"Would you like to try?" he offered.

"You bet your bamboo shoots, Shanghai Shing!" Kareena Leena exclaimed as she popped a piece of squishy pink gum into her mouth and started chomping away. With a mouth full of pink goo she mumbled, "Dis gum iz de-wishes!"

Then came the gigantic bubble. And I'm not talking any basic bubble. After just a few puffs, it was the size of a softball. Three more blows turned it into a pink beach ball. And after just twelve puffs, I thought Kareena Leena attached herself to a hot air balloon ready for liftoff.

And being the responsible brother, I figured it was my job to pop the bubble before my sister flew away. Ok, that's a fib. I really just wanted to see that monster bubble splat all over my sister. Without Kareena Leena knowing, I pulled out my pocket knife and ever so gently poked the bubble's exterior. **Sneaky. Sneaky!**

The bubble instantly exploded with such force that I thought a bomb went off in Shanghai Shing's basement. Murphy grabbed a white towel and waved it as if surrendering to an enemy, and I dove behind a samurai shield waiting for what felt like a tornado to pass. When I looked up, there stood my sweet little sister trapped inside a bubble gum cocoon unable to move a muscle.

"I need a little help here, boys! This caterpillar isn't planning on turning into a butterfly any time soon so get me out of here," Kareena Leena pleaded.

And in that instant, we knew how to catch the Big Apple Bandit. It was a perfect plan, especially since we already knew he loved bubble gum. It was time to set the trap.

CHAPTER 10

# Setting The Trap

It was Go Time. Like Navy SEALs, we needed preparation for battle on land, in the air and in the sea. I started training my troops right there on the spot.

"Give me 20 pushups, Kareena Leena and Murphy!" I screamed. "It's time to build your biceps, train your triceps, and quicken your quadriceps." **Feel the Burn!**

Based on Murphy's puny arms, he hadn't done a pushup in his entire life and Kareena Leena thought pushups had more to do with ice cream than physical exercise.

"Ok, scrap the pushups," were my words as I became more realistic. "Let's just figure out where to put all the bubble gum around the city."

Murphy already had the plan. Once he regained his ability to breathe from his pitiful 2 ½ pushups, he whipped out one of his famous <u>coordinate grids</u>. "I divided the city into roughly 20 sections. It is my hypothesis that if we evenly spread out 25 pieces of chewing gum in the three most travelled areas of the

**Coordinate Grid** (noun): *A fancy way of saying special spots on a map*

city, we have a 75% probability that the Big Apple Bandit will notice a piece of gum within the first four hours of our experiment."

I know I give Murph a hard time about being a little nerdy, but he's the most organized kid I know. For Christmas, most kids wish for roller skates, video games, or a new bike. Not Murph. Every year, he skateboards to the local office supply store and dreams of a new stapler, hole punch, or in his wildest dreams a laminating machine.

My orders involved patrolling all the New York City waterways. That meant placing pieces of bubble gum along the Hudson and East Rivers. Captain Pottsniggle could help me pass out gum to all the boats in the New York Harbor. My base camp was inside Lady Liberty's

**Panoramic** (adjective): *an unbroken view as far left and right as your eyeballs can see*

torch where I had a <u>panoramic</u> view of all the water.

Murphy's orders required him to patrol everything on land. We knew Mr. Mushtaq would love to help and he radioed every New York City taxi cab to be on the lookout for the Big Apple Bandit. **10-4, Good Buddy!**

And finally, Kareena Leena's orders sent her to the top of the Empire State Building. There, she could monitor the New York City skyline from high above. We decided that every bubble gum trail should lead to the Empire State Building's observation deck. That's where the bandit would blow his biggest bubble for all the city to see, unknowing that he would be a victim of his own bubble blowing success.

Kareena Leena requested a minute before we manned our battle stations. "You guys, know I love you," she uttered as tears started running down her cheeks. "We all need to make it out of this alive. You see, I have a 50% off coupon to Saks Fifth Avenue and all of their shoes are on clearance. I can't imagine missing out on those kind of savings."

Before departing, we loaded our backpacks with key supplies: water, food rations, a compass, extra bubble gum, walkie talkies, and, of course, Kareena Leena threw in an extra tube of lip gloss.

**Strategic** (adjective): *Being extra thoughtful about your actions; it's hard for kids when one minute you think about ice cream and the next you think about unicorns.* We quickly scattered bubble gum throughout the city at the most strategic locations. And then we waited, and waited, and waited. **Boring!**

Everything was going according to plan when we hit a snag at Rockefeller Plaza, a famous tourist spot for visitors wanting to ice skate and also see some famous television shows. Murphy noticed that someone skated over the piece of gum on our bubble gum trail that went through the rink. It stuck to her ice skate and disappeared. If one piece of bubble gum went missing, our trail to the Empire State Building would be ruined!

And timing couldn't have been worse when Kareena Leena radioed to all of us. "Bandit spotted one block west on 50th Street approaching Rockefeller Center dressed in all black and blowing a small bubble."

Thankfully, Murphy was in the area and Mr. Mushtaq

zipped him over to the Rockefeller Center skating rink. Murph rented the last pair of skates which just so happened to be fuzzy and purple, his least favorite color. Murph didn't know how to skate but slid, slipped, glided and crashed his way to the center of the rink in time to replace the missing bubble gum and return to dry land. And that's when he heard an eerily familiar voice.

"Hey, Chicken. Freeze!" yelled the voice. Murphy turned just in time to duck and avoid a death grip from Muscles McGuire.

In a moment of courage, Murphy roared, "I beg your pardon, McGuire. I may have skinny legs but I'm not a chicken! We need your help. We're trying to save this city from the Big Apple Bandit!"

You could tell Muscles McGuire was still "steaming" mad from the hot coffee spill, but his girlfriend Roxy chimed in. "Ah, c'mon, Muscle Poo. These kids are trying to save the city. Quit giving them a hard time or you can make your own low-fat banana almond muscle protein shake." Whoa, those were threatening words to a body builder. Foxy Roxy was now on our team.

Like a little puppy dog, Muscles McGuire agreed to help after Foxy Roxy's threat. Adding Muscles McGuire to our team would really help. As an official mall cop, he had big time experience tracking people, mainly teenagers who stole all the napkins from the food court or kids who tried fishing all the coins out of the fountain.

Another message from Kareena Leena echoed in our radios. "The Bandit is paying for rental skates. Get the heck away from the rink or you'll be spotted!"

Murph fled to Mr. Mushtaq's taxi along with Muscles McGuire and Foxy Roxy in the nick of time. The Big Apple Bandit hopped on the ice, performed a very graceful toe loop jump, and then grabbed the bubble gum at center ice. He popped it into his mouth, chewed it up, and blew the classic beach ball size bubble. Our plan was working!

**Jimmy Dinkledine**
(proper noun):
*If you haven't read*
*The Hunt for the Rocky*
*Mountain Marmot,*
*you need to. Jimmy*
*Dinkledine is the spoiled*
*rich kid who tried to ruin*
*the adventure. Tell your*
*mom to buy it online.*

CHAPTER 11

# Behind the Mask

The bandit finished his time at the Rockefeller Ice Rink with an <u>agile</u> double loop jump and then turned in his rental skates. In no time he'd

> **Agile** (adjective):
> *Able to move quickly, like a water bug or naughty kid running from a spanking*

be grabbing an elevator to the top of the Empire State Building.

In the meantime, Captain Pottsniggle ferried me back to the Manhattan shoreline. While sitting in the ship's bridge, I started thinking about the Big Apple Bandit. Was he really an evil villain? Or was he just a normal dude looking for some attention? Just then, I had a sick feeling in my gut. It was that feeling you get when you're lying in bed at night right before you barf. I started wondering if the Big Apple Bandit could be...no way... it couldn't be...but my mind just kept coming back to.... <u>Jimmy Dinkledine</u>. **It Can't Be True!**

I didn't want to believe it, not after all we'd been through chasing the Rocky Mountain Marmot in Colorado. I thought Jimmy learned his lesson about always being true to yourself. But maybe something happened. Maybe he was jealous of our trip to New York. Maybe by stealing the New Year's Eve ball Jimmy thought he could stop time and control the world.

I radioed Murphy and Kareena Leena. "This is Soon-to-be-Famous Amos, over. I have a bad feeling about the Big Apple Bandit. Watch the way he moves, the way he walks, the way he chews his gum. A story of betrayal may be unfolding. I'm afraid the bandit could be... Jimmy Dinkledine!"

"No way, José," Kareena Leena responded. "He can't be the Big Apple Bandit. His fashion colors are blues that are fresh, colorful and lively, not black."

We all knew what Jimmy was capable of. He had more money than Fort Knox and would do anything for attention.

> **Fort Knox**
> (proper noun):
> *A special Army base in Kentucky where soldiers with bazookas guard most of the United States' gold*

As the Big Apple Bandit strolled down 5th Avenue, my heart thumped as we approached yet another possible showdown with Dinkledine. Captain Pottsniggle dropped me off near Battery Park and Jamaica Samuel was there waiting with his bicycle rickshaw. He sensed my fear.

"Relax, my young friend. When hurry-canes hit, New Yorkers clean up. When World Trade Center fall, New Yorkers rebuild. Courage, not cowardice, me brother!"

Samuel launched his rickshaw with a wheelie and in two minutes we arrived at the lobby of the Empire State Building. While Kareena Leena waited on the top floor singing *New York, New York* by Frank Sinatra, I grabbed a newspaper and waited.

Sure enough, two minutes later the Big Apple Bandit entered the lobby and headed straight for a piece of bubble gum sitting next to the elevator door. He unwrapped it, popped it into his mouth, and hopped in the next elevator just as the doors opened.

Murphy, Muscles McGuire, and Foxy Roxy immediately flew into the lobby after being delivered by Mr. Mushtaq once again. Muscles McGuire flashed his plastic mall

cop badge to the police officer on duty allowing all of us to jump to the front of the line. We were on the heels of the bandit and ready to run backup for Kareena Leena.

As you may guess, when the Big Apple Bandit hopped off the elevator, Kareena Leena was in La-La Land. Kareena Leena had run out of patience and drifted into her own imaginary Broadway musical. It was called *New Fork, New Fork*, a love story about a beautiful spoon being <u>courted</u> by a new fork in town. Well, a jealous knife challenged the fork to a dual and both were fatally wounded. The knife and the fork both died and a handsome dish ended up running away with the spoon.

> **Courted** (verb):
> *pursuing someone in a romantic way hoping he or she will marry you. Gross!*

With Kareena Leena distracted, the bandit casually approached the final piece of bubble gum without being noticed. He unwrapped the juicy piece of heaven and you got it, started blowing a bubble. Shanghai Shing said a good twelve puffs would inflate the gum to the size of a hot air balloon, but the Big Apple Bandit kept blowing, and blowing, and blowing. **Oh My!**

After thirty puffs, the bubble grew to the size of a blimp and could be seen throughout the city. New Yorkers were familiar with King Kong climbing the Empire State building, but no one had ever seen anything like this. Some thought it was a pink jellyfish without its

stingers. Others thought one

> **Veered** (verb):
> *A car veers or swerves on the road when a deer runs in front of it. Oh, dear!*

of Jupiter's moons <u>veered</u> off course and landed in the Big Apple, while many children instinctively cheered, "That's not trouble, it's just a giant bubble!"

Before this went too far, Murph handed me a contraption he rigged up during the elevator ride. The device was some type of plastic pipe that shot toothpicks left over from Kareena Leena's karate purse chop. "You know what to do," he quietly uttered.

> **Mayan** (noun):
> *Central American Indians who lived from A.D. 250 to 900 who were so smart they created their own language*

I sure did. If I waited any longer, the Big Apple Bandit might lift off, catch a wind current to New Jersey, and once again escape me bringing him to justice. I loaded my single barrel blowgun and aimed dead center of the bubble. Like an ancient <u>Mayan</u> hunter, I inhaled a deep breath and forcefully blew into my weapon. The toothpick projectile blasted out the end and drove deep into the heart of the massive bubble. **Ka-Pow!**

Pink chunks exploded everywhere and wrapped the Big Apple Bandit in a pink goo cocoon. We surrounded him from all sides. Muscles McGuire pulled out a Taser gun ready to zap the victim into electric oblivion, but Kareena Leena came to the rescue.

"Hey, this naughty bandit deserves to be treated the way you and I would like to be treated," she stated. "Let's be friends," and she slowly reached down to remove the bandit's mask.

"No, Kareena Leena," I screamed. "He may be armed and dangerous!" But it was too late. The mask was coming off. I prepared to see the evil face of Jimmy Dinkledine or even some dirty New York mobster. And to my surprise...

CHAPTER 12

# Ticker Tape Parade

Beneath the mask of the Big Apple Bandit was a... girl! And it wasn't some freaky smelly girl with cooties. It was a girl who smelled good and was actually kind of cute, but I'd deny that if anyone asked me if I think girls are pretty.

Muscles McGuire lunged at the Big Apple Bandit with a pair of handcuffs he borrowed from a real police officer. "Whoa, whoa there, woman! Why don't I whisk you away to some wicked Pwison." He meant to say prison, but Muscles has a cute little lisp and words don't always come out right.

"Hold on," I interrupted. "You're not cuffing anyone. First, she's covered in bubble gum goo, and we can't even reach her hands. And second, I can tell she's scared."

Tears formed in the eyes of The Big Apple Bandit. She looked away from all of us in shame. Moments ago, I prepared myself for a fight to the death, but now I felt sorry for this girl who didn't seem mean at all. And so I asked for her name.

"My name is Trixie, and I'm so sorry for what I've done. I'm not a villain. I just want time to stand still. I'm a kid who found out her dad took a new job in Punxsutawney (pronounced "Pux-ca...oh forget it; it's way too hard), Pennsylvania and I'm afraid of moving to a new city. I feel like a coward."

As Trixie further explained, her dad worked at the Bronx Zoo for twenty years. He recently won the Nobel Prize for Critter Care for the way he's provided for the zoo's twelve ground hogs. When the mayor of Punxsutawney found out, he offered him the job of Official Keeper for Punxsutawney Phil, the world's most famous groundhog.

Every February 2nd, Punxsutawney Phil wakes from hibernation, stumbles outside, and if he sees his shadow, the world knows winter will last another six weeks. Because Punxsutawney Phil is a celebrity, he requires a lot of attention like a special diet, regular brushing, and occasional plastic surgery so his wrinkles don't show up on television.

Kareena Leena chimed in next. "There, there, my little sweetie. Turn that frown upside down and let's get all this pink gunk off of you so us girls can have a chat."

Normally shy, it was actually Murphy who consoled Trixie the most. Girls usually spook Murph a little, but he still managed to talk. "Uh, Trixie, uh. I get scared sometimes. Um, well, I get scared a lot and some people say I'm a coward. But, well, I'm learning that life isn't any fun as a coward. And when I muster up some courage, it's actually pretty great."

Watching all of this, Foxy Roxy was so touched by our compassion that she called her Aunt Hazel who is the secretary to the mayor of New York City. "Aunt Hazel, you'll never believe this. Three kids just saved New

York City from the Big Apple Bandit. And rather than throw her in jail, they made friends with her."

"I have an idea, Trixie," Kareena Leena said with excitement. "How about we all be pen pals? You can write about Punxsutawney Phil the groundhog, and I'll tell you about my dog Doodle."

"Well, I guess I could try, and maybe living near the world's most famous groundhog might be fun," Trixie replied with a gleam of hope in her eye.

Just then, Foxy Roxy's phone rang. It was the mayor and he asked to speak to me. "Hello, this is Amos Fogley."

"Hello, Mr. Fogley, this is Mayor Blabberjabber and I'd like to thank you for saving New York's New Year's Eve Ball. As an expression of my deepest gratitude, I'd like to throw you a parade today at 1:30pm. New York City heroes always receive a New York size parade!"

First, Mayor Blabberjabber asked us to return the New Year's Eve Ball to Times Square. And second, he insisted we bring Trixie to the parade. The mayor loved kids and said we all need second chances.

And so later that day, we received a key to the city, a ride down Main Street in the mayor's limousine, and a free coupon to Marco's Munchies, home of the world's biggest double-decker pastrami and corned

beef sandwich. (I'll make sure this one isn't left in a submarine☺).

After the parade, we headed back to my cousin's house. Dad said we needed some down time after saving the city, so we settled in and watched the latest episode of *Global Gallopers.* Dr. Giggles was in Washington D.C. and it looked like he rigged up some time machine and was heading back in time.

"Hey, guys," I said with a glimmer in my eye. "Anyone want follow Dr. Giggles to...?"

"Hold it right there, Amos," Murphy interrupted. "My bladder just stopped tingling."

But it was too late. We were off on another adventure.

# Acknowledgements

*Many thanks to my literary peeps, including...*

The Bookworm Buddies from
Whispering Meadows Elementary

Mrs. Arch for opening her classroom doors
to a weird dad

Spang-A-Lang-A-Ding-Dong and your passion
for plot

The Fireman and 100% for helping over
deep dish pizza

My favorite illustrator from Minnesota

The Somersault Group for telling the world

# About the Author

David Long is an unashamedly average guy who once again proves that ordinary people, who take a leap of faith, can do extraordinary things. As a child growing up in Toronto, his imagination carried him all over the universe including plate appearances in Yankee Stadium and frequent missions to the moon.

He has been a high school basketball coach, motivational speaker, missionary, college professor, freelance writer, operations manager for two companies and still has no clue what he wants to do when he grows up.

David now resides in Fort Wayne, Indiana where his life looks a lot like yours. In his "free time," he helps with homework, mows the yard, pays bills, threads fishing hooks, flirts with his wife, and eats far too many desserts.

Would you like David Long to visit you?

If yes, a portion of your book sales will
benefit a charity in your community.

For more information,
visit dreambigdreamz.com.

# Other Books
# by David Long

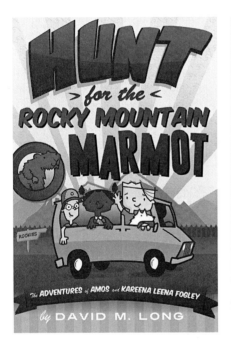

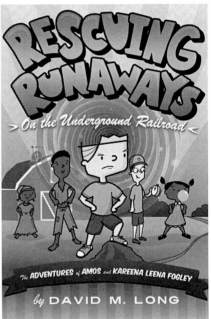